by Antonie Schneider

illustrated by Susanne Strasser

Mr. Happy
& Miss Grimm

Holiday House / New York

One day Mr. Happy moved in next to Miss Grimm—
fence to fence, wall to wall, door to door.

Miss Grimm was annoyed.

Mr. Happy set up his house.
Then he planted some flowers—
for spring, summer,
autumn, and winter.
He also planted an apple tree.

Every morning
Mr. Happy greeted the sun,

every evening the moon
and the stars.

He greeted the rain when it rained,
the snow when it snowed,
and the wind when it blew.

One afternoon Mr. Happy knocked
on Miss Grimm's door.
She opened it just a crack.

"What do you want?" she asked sharply.
"Allow me to introduce myself," he said.
"I'm Happy."
"I'm not," said Miss Grimm.
And she slammed the door in his face.

Mr. Happy returned to his garden,
where he sowed seeds, planted plants,
tilled the soil, pruned shrubs
and trees, and cut the grass.
All the while, he whistled along
with the birds.

Miss Grimm secretly watched
from her window.
"Why is he doing that?"
she wondered.

Miss Grimm began to feel that
something strange was taking over
her bleak little home.
She thought long and hard
about how to stop it
but couldn't come up with a plan.

Meanwhile, the sun shone brightly
in Mr. Happy's garden.
"How splendid to be alive,"
Mr. Happy sang.

Mr. Happy took pleasure in everything:
the black cat next door, the moles,
and even the earthworms.

Once when Mr. Happy saw Miss Grimm in her yard, he waved to her congenially. Seeds flew out of his hands and scattered everywhere.

The wind blew some of them into Miss Grimm's yard.
"What's all this?" Miss Grimm complained.

Day after day wonderful plants grew
beyond Miss Grimm's fence.
They grew bigger and stronger.

Then one day
when Mr. Happy wasn't home,
his garden got out of control.
A shocked Miss Grimm watched
as it happened.

Two enormous sunflowers grew
over her and Mr. Happy's houses
and pushed the two little buildings together.
When Mr. Happy returned,
he took Miss Grimm by the hand,
and she wasn't even annoyed.

As no one who lives under a giant sunflower
can continue to be glum and gloomy,
Miss Grimm decided to change her name.
Today she is called Miss Bliss.

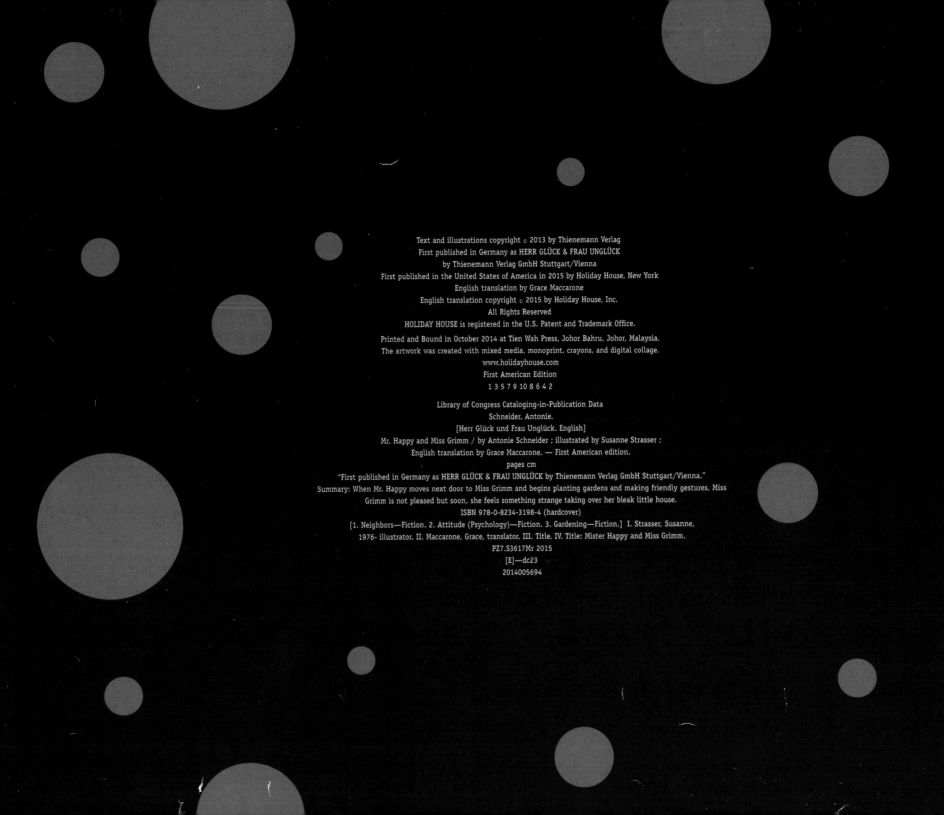

Printed and Bound in October 2014 at Tien Wah Press, Johor Bahru, Johor, Malaysia.
The artwork was created with mixed media, monoprint, crayons, and digital collage.
www.holidayhouse.com
First American Edition
1 3 5 7 9 10 8 6 4 2

Library of Congress Cataloging-in-Publication Data
Schneider, Antonie.
[Herr Glück und Frau Unglück. English]
Mr. Happy and Miss Grimm / by Antonie Schneider ; illustrated by Susanne Strasser ;
English translation by Grace Maccarone. — First American edition.
pages cm
"First published in Germany as HERR GLÜCK & FRAU UNGLÜCK by Thienemann Verlag GmbH Stuttgart/Vienna."
Summary: When Mr. Happy moves next door to Miss Grimm and begins planting gardens and making friendly gestures, Miss
Grimm is not pleased but soon, she feels something strange taking over her bleak little house.
ISBN 978-0-8234-3198-4 (hardcover)
[1. Neighbors—Fiction. 2. Attitude (Psychology)—Fiction. 3. Gardening—Fiction.] I. Strasser, Susanne,
1976- illustrator. II. Maccarone, Grace, translator. III. Title. IV. Title: Mister Happy and Miss Grimm.
PZ7.S3617Mr 2015
[E]—dc23
2014005694